A Hungry Heart

A Seven Fallen Hearts Story

Amanda Hocking

Seven Fallen Hearts 3

This is a work of fiction. All of the characters, organizations, and events portrayed in this novel are either products of the author's imagination or are used fictitiously.

ISBN: 9798878275729

www.HockingBooks.com

Other Books by Amanda Hocking

Seven Fallen Hearts
Virtue
Tristitia
A Hungry Heart
Superbia (Coming Soon)

My Blood Approves Saga
My Blood Approves
Fate
Flutter
Wisdom
Swear
Letters to Elise (Prequel Novella)
Little Tree (Short Story)
My Blood Approves: Complete Saga (eBook Bundle)

Trylle Saga
Switched
Torn
Ascend
Frostfire
Ice Kissed
Crystal Kingdom
The King's Games: A Short Story
The Lost City
The Morning Flower
The Ever After

Watersong Saga
Wake
Lullaby
Tidal
Elegy
Forgotten Lyrics: A Short Story

The Hollows
Hollowland
Hollowmen
Hollowland: Redux
Hollowmen: Redux
Hollow Stars
Into the Hollow Dark
Into the Hollow Horde
The Hollows: A Graphic Novel

Valkyrie Duology
Between the Blade and the Heart
From the Earth to the Shadows

Stand Alone Novels
Freeks
Bestow the Darkness

CHAPTER ONE

THE GRAND DINING HALL IN THE PALACE of the kingdom of Insontia was packed with the nobility and honored guests who had stayed on after the Princess's wedding the night before. The table was overflowing with a sumptuous breakfast feast, and Gula had happily piled his plate up. He was seated only a handful of places down from King Adriel, and that left him with access to some of the finest delicacies the entire lands of Cormundie had to offer.

Last night, Gula's best friend Maxon had married Princess Lily, and this was meant to be the grand banquet to see them off before they left on their honeymoon. But in the middle of the meal, one of the guests had asked for their help in her seaport kingdom, and the new Prince and his bride had rushed off to give her aid.

That left the remaining guests in a somewhat awkward position. The celebration had been put on hold with the absence of the newlyweds – even if it was a temporary one – and an uncomfortable silence had fallen over the hall.

When the door opened, everyone looked up expectantly, some even rising to their feet on the presumption that it would be Lily or Maxon, but instead, it was a surprising member of Gula's brethren, Avaritia.

He was well dressed in crisp satin in an ostentatious shade of violet, but it honestly suited the sharp contours of his handsome face. Around his waist, he wore an ornate braided belt, and a glittering wand was holstered onto it. Ava had been yawning as he sauntered in, but he froze when he noticed everyone staring at him.

"Am I not allowed here?" Ava asked. "The Prince did invite me."

"No, no, come in, come in." King Adriel gestured for him to join them at the table. "The Prince and Princess are otherwise occupied at the moment. They shall return shortly, and the celebration has no reason to wait on them."

Everyone moved into motion then, returning to their earlier revelry and consumption. Across from Gula, a viscount had left early, and Ava took the empty seat. On either side of Gula were Wick (the Princess's witchy godmother) and Aeterna (an irin friend with a pair of feathered wings).

As Ava settled in, he cast an uneasy gaze around at the other guests, and it grew into a glower when his eyes lingered on Aeterna.

"I didn't expect to be seeing you again," Wick told Ava, matching his disapproving glare with one of her own.

"And *I* didn't expect to be here again," Ava admitted with a wry smile. "But the Fabula Inn had nothing in the way of food, and I wasn't about to waste away in my drab room, so here we are."

He'd loaded up on fruits and cheeses as he spoke, and he finished by stealing a particularly scrumptious plum pastry from off Gula's plate, as was his nature.

"I am happy to see you all the same," Gula said jovially, and he readjusted the floral wreath sitting atop his head. Lily and Maxon had it made for him to wear during their nuptials, but he liked it so much, he wore it still. "This will give us a chance to know each other better."

"Don't you two already know each other quite well?" Aeterna asked, his gaze bouncing between Gula and Ava.

"Irins may love to pal around together," Ava said, "but that hasn't ever really been true for the peccati or even the virtus, for that matter."

Much like the virtu, irins served the Mistress of Light, and they were meant to be guardians of Cormundie, helping to guide it toward good. They appeared human, with the addition of a pair of feathered wings on their back, and they could travel between realms with relative ease.

Since Gula and Ava had long served the Master of Darkness, they had very little to do with irins, but it was safe to assume that Aeterna and his brethren got along much better than the peccati did.

"But that is changing now, and I meant that we could all do with knowing one another better." Gula glanced over at Wick and Aeterna, then he let his attention settle back onto Ava. "Now that we're all on the same side, we should be friendly."

"Are we *all* on the same side, though?" Wick asked, and her keen eyes were only on Ava. She was left waiting for a response, because he'd just taken a bite of a pastry and appeared to be in no hurry to answer.

Gula and Ava were peccati who served an angry daemon, Valefor. He had been their Master until seven weeks ago when the Luxuria had fallen for a virtu and defected from the peccati.

So many things had changed since Gula's Master had been exiled, and all of the kingdoms on the magical lands of Cormundie were left in an unusual

3

state known as the Altering. Animals and nature behaved differently, with weather volatile, birds flying backwards, and even the lightning during a storm had been unusual colors.

Ava finally finished chewing and answered, "If you have food like this on your side, maybe it won't be so bad." He peered into an empty goblet on the table. "What are we drinking here?"

"Apple cider and grape juice," Gula said.

Ava frowned. "Nothing harder?"

"This is a *breakfast*," Aeterna reminded him.

"No, the Avaritia is right," Wick chimed in, sounding disappointed to agree with him.

"Why don't we find a pub, have a drink, and then we'll all have a chat?" Ava suggested and rose to his feet without waiting for anyone to reply.

Chapter Two

THE PUB ON THE FAR SOUTHERN SIDE of the Insontian capital city wasn't quite to the level of dive that Gula was used to at the tavern he frequented back home, the Greasy Goblin. But it was far more comfortable than the rigid formalities of the palace and royal ceremonies.

At least that's how Gula felt, and Wick seemed equally at ease as she relaxed into the distressed booth in the back corner. Gula ordered a pint of mead from the barkeep and then settled back beside her, under the creaking rafters.

On the other hand, Ava and Aeterna wrinkled their noses and wiped down the table with a handkerchief. Some of the patrons eyed the irin with the same disdain that Ava had given him, but the kingdom of Insontia was aligned with the Mistress of Light. Even in seedier places like this pub were tolerant of the irins and virtus, although they weren't quite welcoming.

"Now that we're all having a friendly drink," Ava said after he'd ordered himself harder liquor, "what shall we do with our newfound comradery?"

"Keeping your Master banished isn't enough?" Wick asked in her usual sharp way.

Ava brushed her off. "I was looking for more low-pressure shenanigans. We can save the serious plotting until after we've had a drink or seven."

"You *want* to stay here for several more drinks?" Aeterna questioned him dubiously.

"Yes," Ava said, sounding rather weary as he wiped down the rim of his glass. "I certainly preferred the trappings of the palace, but the company and the spirits left much to be desired." He smiled thinly at that. "Present company included, of course."

"Come now," Gula said, trying to keep his denouement light-hearted.

Over the last few days, he'd become something of a mediator between the virtus and peccati, since Maxon and Lily had their hands full with wedding responsibilities. Now that the festivities were coming to a close, Gula had hoped to be setting aside the role. Of course Avaritia would be the one forcing him into it for even longer.

"Let's play telum," Wick proposed, and the three men turned to look at her. "That's how we bonded back when I was a young witch-in-training. We'd sneak out to the pubs at night and take out frustration on the telum board."

"Perfect." Ava finished his drink in one long gulp, then stood up. "Shall we make it more interesting with a wager?"

"I haven't played in ages," Gula declined. Back at the Greasy Goblin, he had seen many a friendship – and telum board – destroyed over a game, so he tended to avoid it all together.

Ava clasped his hands together in front of his face and smirked as he pretended to think. "What should we wager when none of you have anything I want?"

"How about my wand?" Wick asked, pointing to the glittering unicorn horn wand sheathed on his hip.

Ava frowned as he glanced down at it. "I already possess that."

"But you don't know how to use it," Wick countered with an arched eyebrow.

"That doesn't mean I wish to part with it," Ava replied.

"A life of unuse is a waste of such a magnificent thing," Wick said, sounding genuinely sorrowful about the whole situation. "So let's use the wager to make it worthwhile. If I win, the wand returns back to me. If you win, I'll teach you how to actually use it."

Ava considered, then nodded, and when the witch held out her hand, he shook it.

With the wand on the line, Gula and Aeterna decided to watch from the sidelines, nursing their drinks. The octagonal telum boards were on the other side of the pub, where the lanterns hung a bit lower as to more illuminate the area. Signs on the wall warned against cheating, and the clientele apparently took the game very seriously.

Wick and Ava managed to find an empty board, probably thanks to the early hour, and Gula and Aeterna pulled up stools next to them.

"How did you get that wand anyway?" Gula asked as Ava and Wick gathered the sharp telum bolts, before they would take turns tossing them at colored diamonds on the board. "I never did hear that story."

"I lent it to Maxon, and somehow, it found its way into Ava's hands almost immediately."

"As things tend to do," Ava said drolly. "But I assure you that I got it from Lux – *Maxon* – by honorable means. I saved his life, and he repaid me with the wand."

The Luxuria had recently given up the title he'd received from his former Master, and he'd returned to using his birthname. None of them had been close, but it made sense that Ava might still forget the name change after knowing Maxon as Lux for decades.

Gula sipped his mead and watched Ava and Wick play, and he'd been invested in it until he felt a strange warmth on the back of his neck.

He ran his hand through his thick black hair and checked his neck for a fire beetle. But there was nothing, and the warm feeling didn't actually hurt, not like a fire beetle bite would.

"Aeterna!" someone shouted from behind them, and both Gula and the irin turned to look.

Rushing through the pub, crowded because of the wedding tourism, was the most beautiful man that Gula had ever seen.

His dark eyes were framed by long lashes, and he had a full serious mouth, with a hint of a beard tracing his sharp chin and above his upper lip. His hair was silken and the color of sunlight, landing just below his shoulders.

A solitary gold chain hung around his neck, laying on his chest bare from the deep neck of his shirt, and a vest hung snuggly on his shoulders. He was short, maybe an inch or two shorter than Wick, and his ears came to a slight point, meaning at least one of his parents had been elven.

Despite his small stature, the beautiful man pushed effortlessly through the crowd. His eyes were fixed on Aeterna, whose feathered irin wings made him easy to spot.

"Aeterna!" he shouted again.

It took a surprising amount of effort to pull his gaze away from the handsome man rushing toward them, but Gula managed to glance back at Aeterna.

"You know him?" Gula asked in hopeful surprise.

But before the irin could answer, there was a crash. The beautiful man had bumped into a pair of brutish pugilists playing telum, and they whirled on him in a rage.

Without thinking, Gula lunged to his feet and rushed over, arriving with only enough time to block a punch before it was thrown.

"There is no need to go straight to violence," Gula told the pugilists with a friendly smile. "With all there is to celebrate, certainly we can behave as gentlemen."

"Some spoiled maiden's married, and I'm expected to let a shiny elf disrespect my game?" One of the pugilists sneered. "Hardly seems right."

"Then let me share my celebratory mood with you," Gula said, and he spoke louder so that all the pub's patrons could hear. "The next round of drinks are on me!" Everyone cheered, and even the pugilists seemed to relax. "Now does that seem right?"

They glared at him a moment longer, then they finally turned back to their game of telum.

"Thank you for that," the beautiful man said, and Gula was finally able to greet him.

"No thanks necessary," Gula replied. "I meant every word I said." Somehow, he spoke normally even though his tongue felt too big for his mouth and his heart raced in his chest.

"You have my gratitude anyway," the man insisted, and his voice was soft and velvety.

"Come with me," Gula blurted, and then, he hurriedly amended so he wouldn't sound presumptuous and pushy, "I'm sitting with Aeterna, and I heard you calling his name."

"Yes. Yes, of course." The man blinked rapidly, and his expression turned solemn. "I need to speak with him immediately."

Gula turned and led him back to where they were seated. Wick and Ava had apparently finished their game and pulled up stools beside Aeterna.

"That was awfully generous of you, Gula," Ava commented as they approached, referring to his round of drinks. "Does your friendship with the new Prince afford an allowance?"

"Don't be crass," Gula admonished him.

Aeterna had gotten to his feet to greet the handsome man. "Mod? What is the matter?"

Mod. The irin had definitely called the beautiful man Mod in such a familiar way, and it instantly clicked into place.

"*Moderatio*?" Gula asked quietly, and all at once he felt light-headed.

Mod glanced over at him, his dark eyes holding his for the briefest of moments, and then he looked back at Aeterna.

"There is a new danger," Mod told him urgently. "Our Mistress Luminelle has sent me to you because I require your help."

CHAPTER THREE

IT HAD ONLY BEEN A FEW DAYS AGO that Mod had been summoned by Luminelle. Many, many years had passed since she had even spoken to him, and Mod had been living quietly. His home was in the tranquil island kingdom of Sabrii off the southeastern coast of Cormundie.

His mother had been a devout servant as the last Moderatio, but Mod himself had never taken the mantle quite so seriously. Fanatic devotion seemed to be at odds with the very concept of living in temperance. Still, in the early days after his mother had died, he had been more eager to do as Luminelle commanded, but Sabrii was secluded and peaceful.

As the world slowly changed and became less safe for the virtus across Cormundie, his Mistress called on him less, and Mod filled his life with the elven court of Sabrii alongside his father. Eventually, even when Luminelle did reach out for him, Mod stopped answering.

In recent years, Mod thought of her almost never. Until the Altering spread across the lands. He heard the rumors of Valefor's banishment and that a virtu and peccati had somehow fallen in love.

But none of that mattered in Sabrii. Even the signs of the Altering – birds sang their songs backwards and stars swirled in the night sky – were largely benign. He continued his duties and his life of comfort, and he worried very little.

That all changed a few days ago when Mod was
working the courtyard behind his father's home,
pruning the persimmon trees that had become unruly
in the unseasonable warmth of late.

"Moderatio, my servant, my child." Luminelle's
voice came so clearly, he turned around, half-
expecting to find her standing right behind him.

But she was nowhere to be seen.

"Aren't I more of a great-great-great-great
grandchild?" Mod asked and turned his eyes toward
the sky.

When she spoke to him this way, her words
travelling through the ether, she could hear him even
in the other realm.

"You were created from me, as such you are my
child, and I need you," Luminelle persisted, and for
the first time, he heard the desperation in her voice. "I
cannot travel to you, so you must come to me."

Mod lowered his gaze and let his long hair fall
forward. "Mistress, forgive me, but I have obligations
here –"

"One of my irins will be there imminently to
chauffeur you," she said, and no sooner than that,
Mod heard the flap of wings.

He glanced over his shoulder to see one of his
Mistress's powerful guardian irins.

"You're my ride, I presume?" Mod asked, and he
let the irin pull him into his strong arms before they
took flight.

Traversing across realms always made Mod
nauseated, and as soon as he stepped foot in the plush
grass that surrounded Luminelle's palace, he hunched
over and tried to calm his stomach.

"Aren't virtus impervious to air sickness?" the
guardian irin asked rather snidely.

"You can't believe everything you hear," Mod said as he straightened back up. "Cormundie is lousy with rumor and legends, and not all of them are true."

Mod couldn't recall the last time he'd been in his Mistress's palace, but he still remembered the pathway to her garden atrium through the open pillars.

He found Luminelle tending to large acacia plants covered in vibrant yellow blossoms. Her silken black hair was plated with gold thread down her back, and her ivory gossamer gown shimmered against her tawny skin.

As he approached, he'd hoped she would turn around to greet him, but she waited in silence for him to address her first.

"My Mistress, you summoned me?" Mod said uncertainly.

"Am I yet your Mistress?" she asked, still not looking at him.

"Of course you are. I am born of your blood, and I swore my fealty to you," he insisted. "I have been busy because the kingdom of Sabrii has needed me."

"All of Cormundie needs you," Luminelle said sharply and finally looked back at him with her dark eyes.

His throat felt dry, and his words came out weaker than he meant them to when he replied, "I am here now."

"I wasn't sure that you would come," she said, as if she had given him any choice, and she finally smiled and held her arms open to him. "I am so happy to see you, Moderatio."

He stepped into her arms and let her hug him close. As he leaned into her, he realized how much he'd missed her approval and the comfort of a motherly embrace.

When they finally parted, she put a gentle hand on his face and looked down at him, "You look well. Has your quiet life been kind to you?"

"It has," he admitted, but he was quick to change the subject away from any dereliction in his duty. "You didn't invite me here just to tell me how good I look, did you?"

"No," she admitted grimly. "I would not have broken your self-imposed isolation if it were not important. You and some of the virtus have pursued safety in anonymity, and I truly do not wish to see my children in peril."

Mod was not the only virtu who had been living in relative seclusion. His mother had worked visibly as the Moderatio until her dying breath, but even then, she had been one of the few who went by her name outright. Humilitas and Caritas had been hidden so long his mother had never even met them, and Mod himself had only once met Industria and Gratia.

Long ago, the virtus had worked and lived out in the open, the same as the peccati. Even back then, there had been some risk to it, of course. Angry servants of Valefor would attack them, but conversely, pious servants of Luminelle revered them and gave them aid.

Until a horrible disaster struck all of Cormundie several millennia ago. The Golden Blight left plants withering in golden dust, and starvation, death, and rampant violence followed in its wake.

The countrymen turned against the virtus, who could not save them from such a devastating phenomenon. Valefor seized upon the unrest, goading the beleaguered inhabitants of Cormundie, and paying them with food and jewels to harass the virtus. The virtus survived, but they were spit upon, physically attacked, and shunned, even in their own kingdoms.

Eventually, the Golden Blight did end, but the respect and reverence of the virtus had gone along with it. It had become easier and safer to live quietly, doing good where they could without the burden of their name and title.

That was how Mod lived. As the son of an elven lord, he could not be as unknown as he wanted, but most of his kingdom did not realize that he was a virtu. He helped the island of Sabrii, and he acted in alignment with Luminelle's morality, even if he was not answering her calls.

That was enough for him.

"What is it that you need of me now?" Mod asked his Mistress.

"I need you to retrieve a cockatrice's golden egg," she said.

Mod shook his head. "That's a very odd request."

"With Valefor's banishment, I am unable to fetch it myself. That is the equity of the Covenant of Cormundie – with no Darkness on the land, there can be no Light." She gave a tight smile, but it wasn't as if she had been the one to do egg-fetching quests before the change in residence.

"That much I understand, but why do you need a golden egg? And why do I need to be the one to get it? We have no dragons in Sabrii," Mod reminded her.

Cockatrices were the smallest of the dragons – about the size of a wild pheasant – and they were unusual but austere looking little beasts. Their heads were closer to that of a rooster, with golden feather crests and a sharp beaked mouth, but their bodies and wings were covered in leathery scales.

15

They laid eggs infrequently, making them rare, but other than their beauty, they weren't particularly useful.

"A honey cockatrice has made a nest in the Apisius Valley," Luminelle explained. "The valley also happens to be home to the highly venomous megabombus. You, as the Moderatio, are immune to all venoms and poisons, which is why you must be the one to obtain it."

"But what do you need it for?" Mod pressed.

"I need it because Valefor cannot have it," she said. "A golden dragon egg is required to begin the sangcoranimilia."

CHAPTER FOUR

AVA HAD BEEN LISTENING to the elven virtu hurriedly explain why he needed Aeterna to help him steal the unborn young of a cockatrice. But when Mod mentioned the sangcoranimilia, Ava's eyes shot up.

The sangcoranimilia was an ancient ritual so brutal that for a long time, most had believed it was only a myth. But he'd always known it was real, because when magic and humanity combined, the most barbaric things could happen.

Ava didn't know all that was required to execute the ceremony, but throughout the years, he'd gleaned that it included powerful conjuring and a sacrifice of many, many victims. Whoever were to perform it would be able to move about the realms as they wished, no longer bound by the Covenant of Cormundie.

The Covenant was the tenets that had been put in place by Luminelle and Valefor an eon ago, and though Ava had never seen it himself, he understood that it set the rules to how they and their respective minions – the irins and virtus, the sonneillons and peccati – could conduct themselves on Cormundie.

Prior to Valefor's recent exile, there had never really been a reason to perform a taboo ritual like the sangcoranimilia. But the sheer scale of death involved had always left Ava suspicious that the practitioner of the ritual would be granted something much greater than the ability to free roam.

Now it seemed that he might find out for certain.

But Ava couldn't let his face bely the intense fear that struck him at the mere mention of the sangcoranimilia, and he managed a condescending smirk as he leaned back on his stool.

"So they're back on that old rumor again?" he asked Mod in a voice that sounded completely nonplussed.

Mod shot him a look, his sharp eyebrows pinched up. "What do you mean by that?"

"The sangcoranimilia is nothing more than a boogeyman to remind us all the horror that could be inflicted on us," Ava persisted. "But it's too terrible to ever actually be done."

Gula shook his head, and his expression had gone uncharacteristically grim. "Everything has changed, Ava. Valefor has been banished, and this is the only way back. And if your reason for dismissing this ritual is because it's too awful, then that is all the more reason to take this seriously."

"You are against the sangcoranimilia, are you not, Avaritia?" Wick asked pointedly, eyeing him up from across the table.

"Of course I am. A world of devastation and destruction is no fun to live in, and I've never been one to play in filth and ash." Ava leaned forward and rested his arms on the table. "But that's all the more reason we should not get involved with this dragon egg."

Mod glared at him incredulously. "How do you figure such a thing?"

"The cockatrice may be one of the smallest dragons, but she makes a fierce mother," Ava contended. "She's venomous with a hooked stinger on the end of her tail, and she makes her nest in the center of the Aspisius Valley.

"She feasts on the rich honey of the megabombus that also make the valley their home," he went on. "Meaning she has a swarm of them surrounding her, inadvertently protecting her. The egg is far safer with her than it is anywhere else in all the kingdoms of Cormundie."

"That may be true, but the egg will be even safer *away* from here," Mod countered. "If Luminelle has it in her possession in her palace in the other realm, your Master would not be able to retrieve it."

"I have no Master any longer," Ava muttered, but he didn't know how to argue against the virtu except to say that he didn't trust *anyone* with a primary ingredient of the sangcoranimilia.

"I have dealt with the megabombus before," Gula piped up. "I've always had a taste for ambrosian honey, so I have learned how to handle them. I should go with you. I can be of help, if you needed it."

Mod smiled gratefully at Gula. "I certainly could use as much as possible."

There were five of them gathered in the dark corner of the pub – Wick the witch, Aeterna the irin, Mod the virtu, Gula the peccati, and then Ava himself. Yet, Mod and Gula – who had only just met – already looked at one another like they were the only ones in the world.

It was the same way that Luxuria and the Castimonia looked at each other. Ava even thought he'd noticed something charged in the way Tristitia and Industria had spoken last night, though he'd tried to dismiss it as a paranoid imagination.

But now it was unmistakable: there was something transpiring between the virtus and the peccati, and Ava didn't know exactly what it was or why it was happening.

It was with suspicion and fear that he watched Gula and Mod, but it wasn't *only* that.

He'd never admit that it was envy that twisted in his heart. That shouldn't be all that surprising, since he was Avaritia – the greedy, full of unchecked desire and a covetous nature. Even before he'd served Valefor, Ava had always had an insatiable longing for *more*.

So he had filled his life with expensive gems and luxurious clothes, fine wines and rare cheeses, lush beds and immaculate homes.

But no matter how much he had, the yearning deep inside him never ceased. In fact, as of late, it had grown even worse. Every small ember of desire had become a raging inferno.

In the days leading to Valefor's exile, Ava had been more certain than ever that he was meant for something. That he *needed* something else.

"We should all go then, shouldn't we?" Wick was asking, and it drew Ava from his thoughts.

"Mod and I can likely handle it on our own," Aeterna said.

Ava rolled his eyes. "A single irin can hardly handle any threat on their own."

"I thought we were being friendly," Aeterna retorted icily.

"This *is* me being friendly," Ava insisted. "But come now, Aeterna. We've only just now formed our alliance, and you want to split us all up?"

"Are you saying that you *want* to go with us?" Gula asked, surprised.

"Want is not the right word, but there is safety in numbers and all that," Ava said, then looked to Wick.

"Besides, I won the bet and Wick has to pay up with her wand lessons."

CHAPTER FIVE

THE CARRIAGE THAT AVARITIA had booked was extravagant, and that only made Mod more suspicious of the peccati. He hadn't wanted to travel with Ava at all, but Aeterna and Gula had reluctantly vouched for him.

Mod knew he shouldn't put much stock into Gula's words, especially not about his own brethren. And yet Mod *did* value what Gula thought, and he was relieved and excited that he was joining him on this journey.

Within an hour of meeting, they were in this oversized, overdecorated carriage, travelling on the Great South Road to the valley on the western coast, opposite his homeland of Sabrii.

The carriage was larger than most, with a double decker. The main compartment had two plush benches, covered in a velvety damask, and there was even a small cabinet, which housed a few bottles of wine along with fruits and cheeses. An interior ladder on the side led up to the second level. Up there, the ceiling was much lower, but it was decked out with soft pillows and thick curtains, making it a good place to sleep or rest.

Such a large carriage would move very slowly if pulled by the average horse, but this was drawn by a pair of powerful gyltbeests. They were native to the kingdom of Voracitas, and they were the largest antelopes in the land, with long fast legs. Their fur was a shimmering pale apricot, and each animal had a pair of twisting bronze horns protruding from their heads.

Mod had heard the driver promise Ava that a trip that would take a horse-drawn carriage multiple days would be half that by gyltbeest.

Ava and Wick had adjourned to the upper level to discuss something about a wand and a bet, and Aeterna road on the back of the carriage to let his large wings stretch. That left Mod and Gula alone in the main cabin, sitting across from one another.

The attraction between them had been instantaneous and undeniable, but still, Mod planned to deny it. There was too much at stake right now – the fate of the entire world, it seemed – and he could not be distracted because he had met the most gorgeous man he'd ever seen.

The very moment Mod had laid eyes on Gula – when the powerful bear of a peccati had raced to his feet to protect Mod from a feisty pugilist – he had felt a *pull* towards him. Like a tether inside him, drawing him to Gula. But it wasn't until their eyes met that Mod was truly smitten.

Gula's eyes were a deep dark mahogany, and they were as warm and vibrant as the sun. His body was thick and soft, and when Gula faced him, his arms looked so inviting. His smile was timid, almost coy, and he spoke in a cheery baritone.

In the very brief time they had known one another, Mod had been careful not to talk to Gula about anything other than the mission that Luminelle had tasked them with. He hadn't been entirely able to resist looking over at him, but a few stolen glances wouldn't make a relationship.

With three others tagging along, Mod had assumed he would have buffers to keep him from getting to know Gula in any meaningful way. But now they were alone, with the only thing to distract them was the world flying by out the windows, and they were moving too fast for him to see much more beyond a blur.

"How long have you served your Mistress?" Gula asked, breaking the long silence.

"All my life," Mod replied, still staring out the window.

"Of course." Gula laughed, sounding embarrassed. "I forgot that you virtus are born into it."

"I never do," Mod said, but his words came out harsher than he meant. He gave Gula an apologetic smile and asked, "How long have you served your Master?"

"I started over a hundred years ago, but I haven't served him in seven weeks."

"Because he was banished," Mod surmised.

"Before that actually," Gula corrected him with a smile that vacillated between proud and sheepish. "Maxon and Lily may have been the ones to get him exiled, but I helped Maxon. He wouldn't have gotten to Lily without me."

"Maxon?" Mod asked, confused.

"The Luxuria. That's his birth name," Gula elaborated. "But now he's back to Maxon Eromare Regulon, the new Prince of Insontia and former Prince of Desiderium."

"Who were you before you became the Gula?" Mod asked, giving into his curiosity.

"I grew up in Voracitas," Gula said, as if that explained much of anything about who he was.

Voracitis was a kingdom known for its ambrosian honey and gold mines, but that said nothing about an individual.

"Were they cruel to you then, your parents? Is that why you took up with the darkness?" Mod asked.

"No, they weren't cruel. Not at all." Gula shook his head adamantly. "We were poor, and life was difficult. But they laughed a lot, and they loved all of us. I was the youngest of thirteen kids, the real runt of the litter, if you can believe that now." He gestured to his ample frame.

"Were you starving then?" Mod pressed.

"No. We struggled, but we never went without. I was never underfed, but I always wanted more," Gula said. "Not only of food and drink, but all of life. I wanted to try *everything* the world had to offer me. Do you ever feel that way? Do you ever long for more?"

Mod couldn't bear to hold his gaze any longer, so he pretended to pick lint off his trousers. "No, I can't say that I have," he lied, and he instantly regretted it and wished he'd told him the truth.

"*Oh*," Gula replied, defeated.

"I have never lived anywhere but the island of Sabrii," Mod said at length. "I have rarely travelled outside of my own kingdom. For years, the only sights I have seen have been the only ones I have ever truly known." He cleared his throat and looked up at Gula. "Ask me the question again."

"Do you ever long for anything more?" Gula repeated softly.

"Every day," Mod said, and he was surprised to find tears springing in his eyes. "Every single day of my life. But there is work to be done where I am, and

I am needed. So I stay and I work, and the world is better for it."

He blinked back the tears and looked away from Gula. He didn't know why he'd needed to be so honest with him, or why he felt *any* of the things he felt for him.

"It must be such an overwhelming thing to be so far away from home," Gula said gently. He got up and walked across the carriage, and he held out an embroidered handkerchief.

"It can be," Mod admitted and tentatively took the handkerchief from him. "Thank you."

As he dabbed his eyes, Gula sat down beside him and said, "But it must be exciting to finally see the world."

"It is an Altered world," Mod reminded him. "Full of unrest and unknown dangers."

"Yes, there is danger, but there is still beauty," Gula persisted. "There is more to life than being safe."

"I can't argue with that," Mod agreed wistfully, and he pulled his gaze away from Gula's handsome face.

"Why would you even want to?" Gula asked and let out a low chuckle, making Mod's heart flutter.

"I don't know." Mod laughed at his own confusion, but he suddenly thought of his mother. "Growing up, my mother had always told me that the true beauty of life was in what we give the world, not what the world had to give us."

His jaw tensed as he considered her words more deeply. "Perhaps I took it to heart too much. What was meant to be a lesson in generosity has caused me to feel guilt at enjoying the pleasures of life, and of doing any of the things I want to do."

"What is it that you want to do?" Gula asked him thoughtfully.

"I want to see the world." Mod gave him a tired smile, and despite the excitement of the day, he found himself yawning. "But maybe a nap first."

The trip was long, even with the fast gyltbeests, and Gula agreed with his assessment. Mod was exhausted from his travels from Sabrii to Insontia, and now beyond that. Gula had been so busy with wedding celebrations and needed the rest himself, and so they were both soon slumbering on their respective benches.

Mod awoke to the sound of a newsboy shouting, and he realized that they must have arrived in the Golden City. The curtains were drawn so he couldn't see it, and Gula was snoring softly on the bench across from him.

When Mod sat up, he realized that at some point during his sleep, Gula had draped his jacket over him. He smiled to himself and admired the gentle features of Gula's face as he slept, and he hoped he was dreaming of something nice.

Mod pulled back the curtains to take in the legendary Golden City, and he had to squint at the brightness of it. Once his eyes adjusted, he realized it wasn't quite as he'd imagined.

Growing up in a faraway kingdom, he had always heard that the Golden City was dipped in the gold they harvested from Voracitis's mines, but up close, it seemed to be much more exaggerated than he expected. Most of the buildings around them were gilded in bronze, gold, and copper, but a few of them had clearly just been painted yellow.

Abruptly, the carriage stopped, knocking both Mod and Gula onto the floor.

"What's going on?" Gula asked, groggy and startled. "Why'd we stop?"

"Because I stopped us," Ava explained as he climbed down the ladder from the upper level of the carriage.

"Is it time for a meal break?" Gula asked.

Ava had reached the main floor and smoothed out his suit. "You are free to do as you wish, but our paths are diverging here."

"What paths? Aren't you going with us to get the egg?" Mod asked, narrowing his eyes.

"You have it under control, and I have other business to attend to," he replied vaguely and opened the carriage door.

"Ava, what changed?" Gula asked, clearly confused.

"Nothing. My plan was always to split from you when I reached the Golden City, and here we are, so here I go," Ava replied glibly, and he stepped out into the bright sunlight.

Gula called after him again, but Ava quickly disappeared into the crowded streets.

Aeterna came inside the cabin after seeing Ava leave, and Wick came down from the upper level. Both of them found it equally weird the way Ava departed like that, but there wasn't much that any of them could do about it now.

Besides, they didn't have time to waste, in case Ava was attempting to get to it first, which meant that they had to hurry onward without any chance of seeing the city. Mod nibbled on fruit and watched out the window at the bright buildings passing by, and Gula sat beside him, explaining the landmarks, so he still got to see something as they raced through the city.

CHAPTER SIX

THE GYLTBEEST WERE EVEN FASTER than promised, and they reached their destination by the following morning. The driver stopped the carriage at the top of the hill, because there were no roads into the Apisius Valley, and he promised to wait for them there for three days, although he didn't seem optimistic that he would see them again.

From the slopes that surrounded the perilous valley, Gula could see everything, and it was just as he remembered it.

The ground was carpeted with lush grass and wild ferns that grew past his knees, but most of the flora and fauna here were of gigantic proportions. Colorful mushrooms and flowers towered over them like trees, with petals the size of children.

Mod's eyes were wide, and his lips were parted in awe as he admired the scenery. "This is so *spectacular*."

"It is," Gula agreed. "But there are dangers beneath all that splendor."

Even here at the edge of the valley, he could already hear the hum from the oversized jungle. That constant *hum* was really the permeating buzzing of the megabombus echoing through the dense plant life.

The megabombus were not visible through the thick foliage, but they were there, flying just beyond the leaves. Round and fluffy, with contrasting vertical stripes of black and gold, they were adorable cousins of the bumblebee, but that only made them deceptively dangerous.

A fully grown megabombus was the size of a donkey with a six-inch stinger. The tip was like a sharpened knitting needle, and it came with a dose of potent venom that caused agony and temporary paralysis in most living things.

Gula led the way into the valley because he had grown up nearby, and he knew the terrain the best. It had been decades since he'd been back, but he never forgot his childhood, no matter how much time had passed.

"These flowers smell like lemons!" Mod exclaimed in delighted surprise as he inhaled a few bright blossoms.

Gula grabbed him around the waist and pulled him back, just a moment before the delightful blossom sprayed out a viscous liquid.

"The lemondrops spray out an acidic substance whenever they're disturbed," Gula explained. "It'll burn straight through your fabric, or your skin, if you're not impervious."

Even though the threat had passed, Gula's arms lingered around Mod. The virtu's back was pressed up against his stomach, and he could feel his heart racing.

"Thank you for saving my vest." Mod tilted his head, so he could look back at Gula, and then both their hearts were racing in time.

"Nobody's hurt, so shall we keep moving?" Wick suggested.

The witch and the irin had been following behind them, and Gula had actually forgotten them. Sometime when Mod looked at him, he forgot almost everything else in all of Cormundie.

But Wick had interrupted, and now he remembered, and he immediately released Mod and stepped back from him.

Gula cleared his throat and started on again. "Yes, let's get going."

A smaller bombus – only the size of a dairy goat – dipped beneath the canopy, and Mod audibly gasped when he saw it.

"I didn't expect them to be so cute," he added in an excited whisper, and Gula couldn't help but chuckle at that.

"That's why it's always good to remember that danger comes in *all* shapes and sizes," Aeterna said rather sagely.

Despite their mission, all four of them paused for a moment, watching the bombus buzz about on its search for food. A plethoric rainbow of flowers surrounded them, but the bombus seemed indecisive.

It was likely because the flowers were mostly suntraps. They had thick straight stalks like green tree trunks, with a solitary broad flower at the top. Each blossom had a large velvety bed of umber nectar and pollen surrounded by petals. They came in the warm shades of a sunset – yellows, oranges, and reds, so they had somewhat of a sunflower appearance.

"What are those called?" Mod asked, pointing to the flower as the bombus finally landed on one.

"Suntraps," Gula answered.

"Suntraps?" Mod tilted his head in confusion, and gestured to the canopy of green leaves and larger flowers above them that let in only a few slivers of sunlight. "Why are they growing in the shade?"

"They don't need that much sunlight. They just look like the sun, and they –" Gula started to explain, but suddenly, the suntrap flowerhead bent in the middle and snapped shut onto the bombus The nectar made the bug's feet too sticky to lift off quickly, and the petals folded around it, ensnaring the insect.

"Well, and that's the trap part," Gula finished.

"Even the plants are carnivorous here?" Mod asked, clearly alarmed.

"Even before the Altering, the valley was an upside-down place," Wick muttered. "Bees are big, dragons are small, and the flowers will eat you."

"They don't eat humans, or elves, or witches, or really anything other than the bombus or some of the other larger insects," Gula corrected her.

"And not irins, but nothing ever eats an irin," Aeterna said with an immodest smile.

"Still, we ought to find the cockatrice nest by nightfall, and I'd rather not watch the suntrap digest the bombus, so I suggest we keep a move on," Wick said, once again urging them along.

Mod was so enchanted with the surreal environment, and he'd often stop and stare. Gula would've been happy to explain everything to Mod, giving him a personalized tour of the valley, but unfortunately, Wick was right.

Mod had started walking again, but he couldn't help himself, and he had to ask what a bright purple mushroom was called.

"That's an armillaria –" Gula began, but before the words had even left his mouth, he felt something snapping down on his arm.

He'd been looking back over his shoulder, smiling at Mod. Then all at once a suntrap was grabbing him by the arm and lifting him high up into the air.

Aeterna flew up behind him and grabbed him by the legs. Gula thrashed and kicked, but the suntrap had a surprisingly strong grip. As the irin tried to help him, another suntrap snapped at his wings. The plant wasn't strong enough to cause much harm to the irin, but the nectar clung to his feathers. He flapped his wings haphazardly before the nectar weighed them down too much, and he fell to the ground.

Mod held his hands out before him, and a powerful gust of wind whipped through the plants around them as he used his virtu powers to conjure the air.

At first, the suntrap only clamped more tightly onto Gula, so as the wind thrashed the plant around, Gula went with it.

But finally Mod was able to direct a powerful enough burst to bend the suntraps. The hungry flower finally released Gula, and he landed in the grass with a heavy thud.

Mod shouted his name and rushed over to him. Gula sat up slowly and rubbed his aching arm, but honestly the worst part was the nectar all over his hands, so all the grassy debris and dirt from the valley floor stuck to him.

"Are you okay?" Mod knelt beside him, and his eyes were wide with concern. "Did you break anything?"

"No, I'm okay. I just need to clean off my hand." Gula gave him a reassuring smile. "You saved me."

"Of course I did." Mod returned the smile easily. "Why wouldn't I?"

"I thought the suntraps weren't supposed to attack anything other than bugs," Wick complained as she tried to help Aeterna clean the gummy nectar off his wing.

"Well, they definitely aren't supposed to attack me, either," Aeterna grumbled and grimaced as the witch plucked at his feathers. "It must be the Altering."

While the irin had been talking, Gula realized that the buzzing sound was growing louder, loud enough the grass around them began to tremble.

Mod took his hand as they both looked up toward the sky, and they saw a swarm of bombus closing in around them.

CHAPTER SEVEN

WHEN WICK HAD LEFT her cottage a week ago, she had only packed for what she assumed she'd need for Lily's wedding. This impromptu expedition had happened on such short notice, she'd only had time to gather up a few of the potions she'd packed.

As the swarm of megabombus closed in around them, Wick knew that she hadn't brought enough.

She reached into her satchel and grabbed a deflection potion. It was a glittering powder in a small sack, and Wick opened it and threw it at the heart of the swarm. The dust collided with a few of the bombus, and they froze midair for a moment, but quickly recovered.

"Do you have anything more powerful in that satchel?" Aeterna asked.

"No, unfortunately, I hadn't thought to pack my fatal potions when I left for a wedding," Wick replied sourly.

"I mean, it was a wedding between a virtu and a peccati, so it would've been prudent," Aeterna countered, his voice tight with frustration.

"You're both making an excellent argument," Mod interrupted. "But do either of you actually have a plan on how to handle all these?"

"Mod and I are immune to their toxins, but I don't know how any of us will fair with a hundred stingers stabbed into our torso like daggers," Gula chimed in unhelpfully.

"*Apage!*" A woman suddenly shouted, and a bolt of lightening shot through the air and zapped the bombus closest to them.

Apage was an incantation that Wick knew well, one she would've used if she still had her wand. But without the magic of the wand, she would just be a witch shouting into the void.

Immediately afterwards, the bombus began to disperse, and the buzzing retreated with them. The nearby suntraps that had bent low to snap their floral jaws at them slowly straightened back up.

Wick looked back over her shoulder to see who had saved them, and she saw an enchanting woman in a black gossamer cloak standing a few feet away. Her spell had been so powerful that even the grass and thick plant stalks leaned away from her.

Maybe it was the adrenaline talking, because Wick had just felt so close to death, but the woman was breathtaking. Her lashes were long and thick, and her wide mouth was pressed into a knowing smile. Her face held the lines of a woman in her later years, but her hair was dark, and her eyes still held a spark of something spry and wild.

Aeterna broke the silence first as he got to his feet. "Thank you for helping us."

"The bombus are more aggressive than usual, and this is no place for a hike," the breathtaking woman chastised them.

"No, it's not, but we're not on a hike," Mod clarified. "We have important work to do."

"Don't we all?" the woman asked wryly. "I live in a nearby clearing, and you all seem a little worse for the wear. Why don't you come back with me and get yourself cleaned up? I have a stew on at home."

"Thank you," Aeterna said. "We would be very grateful."

The woman raised up her hand to silence him. "Don't thank me yet. You haven't tried my stew." And then she turned and started walking.

"What shall we call you?" Wick asked as she followed her.

"Vasilisa," the breathtaking witch replied, and Aeterna stepped in to make quick introductions.

With Vasilisa leading the way, the flora and fauna didn't bother them. Still, Wick was relieved that it only took a few minutes to reach the clearing.

There, the sunlight broke through the canopy of oversized mushroom caps and fern leaves, and it perfectly illuminated the quaint cottage in the center. The flowers and other dangerous plants had been cleared away, creating a path that led directly to the front door.

The cottage itself looked like it had been pulled directly from the watercolor pictures in a fairy tale that Wick had read as a child. Stones along the pathway were painted to look like gumdrops, and the shutters framing the window were pastel shades of blue and pink.

Even the roof was enchanting. The shingles were made of the scales that dragons shed, coming in iridescent shades of every color in the rainbow, and in nearly as many sizes. From the chimney, the plume of smoke sparkled red and smelled of cinnamon and sugar.

"Is this where you live?" Gula asked.

"Yes, this is where I call home," the woman said with a hint of pride in her voice.

"It's very cute," Mod mused. "It looks like something a wicked witch would make to lure children."

"What an awful thing to say to someone who has only helped us," Wick chastised him.

"Well, he's not entirely wrong," Vasilisa admitted with a crooked smile. "Though the 'wicked' part is inaccurate."

Gula slowed his steps and looked to Vasilisa with new suspicion. "But... you do lure children?"

She walked ahead of them down the path. The others lingered back a bit since her potential confession, but Wick stayed beside her, wanting to see her face when she spoke.

"I *help* children," Vasilisa explained. "When I was a young girl, my family was struggling, and so my stepmother had my father abandon me in the forest to fend for myself. I survived – barely – but Cormundie can be a harsh place to live for a child. Sadly, that story is not uncommon here, especially during times of famine or drought.

"As I grew up, and realized my aptitude for magic, I decided to put my good fortune forward to helping others," Vasilisa said. "So I created a home that is welcoming and safe to others, particularly the lost children."

"That's very thoughtful of you," Wick said with a warm smile.

"The world may be hard, but I don't need to be," Vasilisa replied simply.

When they reached the house, Vasilisa told them that she didn't have any children staying with her now, although she did have a fat baby bombus.

"That's Alba," she introduced them to the striped-baby scurrying about. "Since the Altering, some of the bombus have been born with wings or stingers. They can't survive in the valley on their own, and so I thought I'd give this little one a chance."

Alba ran around and spindly legs, and Gula gave his fluffy head a gently pat. "He's much friendlier than I'd expect, and so soft."

Wick cleaned the nectar from Aeterna's wings, while Vasilisa went into the kitchen to finish preparing the stew for them all to eat.

Mod tended to Gula, and Wick couldn't help but notice the way the two of them looked at each other, and the way Mod's hand lingered on Gula's arm long after he needed it.

It was a strange thing, what appeared to be happening with the virtus and peccati, and she didn't yet know what to make of it.

Later, when the food was cooked, they all sat around the table in the kitchen together. Wick helped as much as Vasilisa would allow, but the other witch seemed to prefer playing hostess to her guests.

"What has brought you out into the valley?" Vasilisa asked over the meal. "You don't seem to be the usual crew in search of ambrosian honey."

"We are not," Wick admitted, but she wasn't sure how much to share, so she took a bite to deflect answering further.

"We're looking for a cockatrice," Mod announced, and Gula looked to him in surprise that he was so forthcoming. "Do you know where they nest?"

"Half-a-day's walk, maybe," Vasilisa said. "Near the coast. But a cockatrice isn't easy to handle. What do you mean to do with her once you find her?"

"We're on a mission for Luminelle, but we mean the dragon no harm," Mod elaborated. "In fact, if all goes well, we won't ever interact with one at all."

"Hmm," Vasilisa replied thoughtfully, but she didn't say anything more.

"How long have you lived out here?" Mod asked her, making conversation after the awkward silence fell.

"I don't keep track much anymore. Twenty years? Maybe longer," Vasilisa said.

"And were you always a witch?" he asked, and both Wick and Vasilisa laughed.

"You haven't met very many witches, have you?" Wick asked him.

He blushed slightly and replied, "There aren't many witches in Sabrii."

"I don't know much about witchcraft, either," Gula chimed in. "How does one become a witch?"

"I was born an average human child, my father worked in the gold mines, my mother was a maid, and she died when I was young," Vasilisa explained. "They thought I was a boy, and they called me Vasil, and they never paid any mind when I'd conjure the air or fire or make a toy levitate.

"After my stepmother abandoned me in the woods, I realized that I was really a Vasilisa, and that I had an aptitude for magic," she went on. "So when I was a teenager, I went to a witchcraftorium. There, I studied witchcraft and truly learned to harness the magic, so I can cast spells and use a wand."

"And what is the difference between a sorceress and a witch?" Gula asked.

"Magic is another element of the natural world, not unlike air and water," Wick supplied. "A witch is simply someone who learns how to channel that element and tap into it, using it to help or to hurt, whichever they choose. But magic itself is a neutral force."

"In contrast to witchcraft, sorcery is about bending magic to your will, tapping into that innate force of the world and using it solely to gain power for oneself and inflict harm on others," Vasilisa elaborated.

CHAPTER EIGHT

AS THE NIGHT SETTLED IN over the valley, Vasilisa offered them all a place to sleep. Wick stayed up, helping Vasilisa with chores and talking, but Mod was exhausted from the day's adventures, and he hoped the beds in the witch's quaint cottage were as comfortable as his at home.

There were only two extra rooms, and Vasilisa had offered Mod and Gula the one at the top of the stairs.

When Mod entered the bedroom, he found it decorated the same as the rest of the house – a whimsical animal mural on the walls, soft drapery hanging over the windows, and pastel blankets covering two single beds.

Or rather, he found Gula hunched over one of the beds, stripping off the blankets and pillows.

"What's the matter?" Mod asked.

"Oh, well, nothing's the matter." Gula shrugged, but his expression turned sheepish. "The bed's just built for little children, and I am no small boy.

"I'm just going to make myself a bed on the floor with the blankets and what not," he went on, as if that would be enough to make the hardwood floor bearable.

"No, no, that won't do." Mod shook his head and went over to start taking the linens off the other bed. "But if we put all pillows and mattresses together right in the center of the room, it just might work."

"What do you mean?" Gula asked, sounding puzzled.

"There's no reason for you to sleep on the floor when we have enough fluff that we can both sleep happily."

"But you can fit on one bed, and you'd have more room to stretch out," Gula countered.

"We've both had a long day, and you shouldn't suffer just because you're built differently than me," Mod insisted, and then something occurred to him, and his cheeks darkened with embarrassment. "Unless what you're saying is that you don't wish to share, and I could always sleep downstairs on the sofa."

"*No*," Gula said quickly. "There will be enough room. You should stay."

He smiled gratefully at him, and together, they created a big, plush bed. At Mod's insistence, Gula laid down first, sighing happily as he stretched out his ample frame, and there was just enough room for Mod to lay down beside him. Their arms had to touch a little, and every time they brushed up against each other, his heart would flutter.

"What was your name?" Mod asked once they were both settled in, because he couldn't sleep until he knew the truth about the man who shared his bed.

"*What?*" Gula laughed tiredly. "I'm Gula. Did you forget my name?"

"No, the name your parents gave you, the one you had before your title became your identity," Mod clarified.

Gula was silent for a moment, long enough that Mod worried he'd fallen asleep or maybe he was upset by his prying.

"Ladon," he said at length, his voice soft and thick. "I haven't said it aloud in… I don't know how long."

"I'm sorry. I didn't mean to make you talk about something you don't want to talk about."

"No, that's not it." He breathed in deeply, and Mod turned to look at him in the dim light of the bedroom. "It felt strange to say, strange but… sweet, like cotton candy on my tongue, gone before I really even taste it."

"Is that a good thing?" Mod asked uncertainly.

"Yeah," he answered slowly. "Gula was never really my name. It was only my title, and it's not anymore, since I'm not serving Valefor. But I don't know if I can be Ladon again."

"You always were, weren't you?" Mod asked. "You can be him again, if you want to. I can call you Ladon or Gula or Gudon, but you're still you."

"I think I like Ladon," he said.

"I think I do, too," Mod agreed.

CHAPTER NINE

LADON. HE WHISPERED IT to himself in the morning when he hunched over to look at his reflection in the pastel mirror in Vasilisa's house.

As far as he could tell, he looked the same as he had before, the same as he had for the past centuries he'd lived as Gula. His smile was wider and irrepreseible, but that was because of Mod, not because he'd claimed his name back for himself.

Although that wasn't entirely true, either. Mod had all but *given* it to him. For so very long, before Valefor had been exiled, Gula had wanted to be something more. He'd thought it was because he had a gluttonous desire that could never fully be satiated.

But now, with his ties severed from any Master or Mistress, and rechristened with the name that his mother had chosen, he felt closer to complete than ever before.

He was Ladon, and he'd always have a hunger for the indulgences that life had to offer, but he could be happy and content.

He was the last one up, and he followed the scent of fresh pastries and fruit teas until he found Mod, Aeterna, Wick, and Vasilisa sitting around the kitchen table. They were discussing their plans for collecting the cockatrice egg after breakfast, and Aeterna was bent over, petting the fluffy wingless bombus, Alba.

"I, *ahem*," Ladon cleared his throat, and he was surprised by how strangely nervous he felt when the four pairs of eyes – five if he counted the baby bombus Alba – looked expectantly up at him.

"Is everything okay?" Aeterna asked, his brows drawn with concern.

"Yes. It is. There's no need to worry," he assured them with an awkward laugh, which only succeeded in making everyone appear even more worried.

Finally, he took a deep breath and announced, "My name is Ladon, and that's the name I'd like to be called. From now on. If it's not too much trouble."

"Of course, it's not too much trouble," Wick said in a way like she had no idea why *anyone* would think it was a big deal.

"I'll be happy to," Aeterna agreed breezily, and Mod gave him a proud smile as he sipped his cup of tea.

Vasilisa walked over to him and put her hand warmly on his arm. "I'm so glad I got to know you better, Ladon."

Once they finished their breakfast, they headed out to finally fetch the golden egg of the cockatrice. Vasilisa promised them that they could return if they needed it, and Wick lingered in the doorway as the witches took their time saying their goodbyes.

Mod paused to grab one of the colorful gumdrop stones from along the path, and he tucked it away in the bag of his belongings he'd brought with them.

"What did you take that for?" Ladon asked.

Mod shrugged. "I just think it might come in handy later on."

Aeterna's wings had returned to form, but he preferred to walk on the ground with the others to help keep guard, and to stay out of the way of bombus and suntraps.

The four of them trekked through the Apisius Valley, and in the afternoon, they reached their destination.

The cockatrice dragon built their nests in the prickly shrubs that surrounded the base of a giant black palm tree. All over the tree trunk were long, spiked thorns, making it impossible to climb and dangerous to even get near it. Vibrant green fronds grew out from the top, from surprisingly sturdy black branches.

In fact, they were so strong, they could support an active hive of megabombus. The hive buzzed so loudly overhead, the air seemed to vibrate with it.

Wick and Aeterna weren't impervious to the cockatrice venom, so they stayed outside the shrubbery to watch for danger. Ladon and Mod crawled under the thicket of spikes and toxic berries, until it closed in so much that Ladon's bulky frame couldn't fit through.

Mod crawled on ahead, and Ladon had to watch apprehensively from a distance as Mod reached the nest.

CHAPTER TEN

THE NEST OF THE COCKATRICE was made of hardened honey and palm spikes, so it more closely resembled a porcupine than a traditional bird nest. On top of it, the cockatrice sat with her tail coiled around her like a snake, but from where Mod was crouched, he couldn't see the egg.

The egg had to be there, because Luminelle had told him so, and he carefully crawled through the briar and branches as soundlessly as he could manage.

It worked, and the dragon was still asleep when he reached the nest. Mod peered over the spikes, and he finally caught sight of the glimmering golden egg. It was nearly the size of its mother, and Mod had no idea how such a small creature could lay such a giant egg.

Mod had never seen a cockatrice – or any dragon actually – in real life, and the paintings he'd seen in books didn't do them justice. The scales across her back shimmered like freshly polished gold coins, and the feathers on her head had a glint of rainbow iridescence to them. Her tail was long and serpentine with a hooked stinger at the end nearly the size of the dragon's head.

As the Moderatio, one of his gifts was being resistant to all venoms and poisons, but the stinger would still hurt if it stabbed into his skin like a dagger. So he still hoped very much to avoid that, and that's why he'd left Ladon in charge of making a distraction.

Just at the edge of the shrubs, Wick and Aeterna began making loud whooping noises, sounding like a hungry bird, and Ladon started shaking the branches on the other side of the nest from where Mod was crouched down.

The cockatrice immediately sat up, and she let out an annoyed hissing sound. Ladon shook the branches and growled, and the cockatrice raised her tail up over her back and hurried out of the nest to investigate and scare off any threats to her egg.

The moment she was gone, Mod hurried to snatch the egg out of her nest, deftly maneuvering between the spikes, and so the cockatrice wouldn't notice it was gone and chase after them, he replaced it with the gumpdrop stone he'd taken from outside Vasilisa's house.

He dropped the egg back into his bag, and he quickly ducked between the branches and made his way out around the back of the tree.

"I got it!" Mod shouted when he'd escaped, so the others could stop trying to distract the cockatrice.

Gula embraced him in his excitement, but they didn't waste any time to celebrate, not when the cockatrice could still come after them, so they all hurried away.

Even though the trip out to the nest had been relatively uneventful – likely thanks to a protection spell that Vasilisa had cast over them – Aeterna insisted on escorting them back to the cottage.

It was early evening when they reached the clearing, and Aeterna stopped at the edge.

"You should be safe from here, and I really ought to get this egg to Luminelle." The irin patted his bag, where the egg was safely stored.

"I'm glad that it'll be safe with her, but it's a real shame we had to take it from the mother," Mod said.

"Once it's hatched, we'll likely give the baby back to the mother," Aeterna assured her. "It's only the egg that works in the sangcoranimilia."

Mod smiled, relieved. "That's wonderful! I hated the idea that I was kidnapping that baby, even if it was for the greater good."

"Thank you for all your help today," Aeterna said, his eyes bouncing over Wick, Ladon, and Mod. "I'm sure I will be seeing you all again soon."

Wick continued ahead to the cottage, seemingly excited to greet Vasilisa, but Mod and Ladon both walked more slowly. With the egg gone, speed was no longer necessary, and they could be more languid in their movements.

But that wasn't the only reason that Mod had slowed. When Aeterna left, he'd been hit suddenly by the realization that all of them would be parting ways soon. He had no reason to stay here any longer, so he would go back to Sabrii.

"I don't want to say goodbye to you," Ladon blurted suddenly, as if he'd been reading Mod's thoughts somehow.

Mod stopped short and blinked at him, and he was too startled to say anything but, "What?"

"I know you're not leaving now, or at least, I think you aren't. We'll probably leave in the morning, I assume, because it's safer," Ladon rambled, and he couldn't seem to meet Mod's gaze. "But soon we'll be leaving, and you're probably set to go back home. And I don't even know if they need you there. But I do know that Maxon needs me here, so…"

Ladon trailed off, then took a deep breath. Finally, he lifted his dark eyes, and they were imploring and desperate as he met Mod's gaze.

"You feel it, right?" Ladon asked thickly.

And then, as if he'd thrummed it with his fingers, like it was a lyre string, Mod felt the *pull* between them intensify, and it was all he could do to keep from running into Ladon's inviting arms.

"I do," Mod admitted without hesitation.

"Something is going on here. Something that feels really big," Ladon continued. "And I want to know you. I want to be with you. I want to figure out whatever this is *together*."

He chewed his lip for a moment. "Is that crazy? Am I asking for too much?"

Mod shook his head, and he meant to say no. He meant to tell him that he understood every word Ladon had said, but he couldn't resist anymore, and he could see all over Ladon's face that he didn't want him to.

Mod closed the distance between the two of them, and he pushed himself all the way up on his tiptoes. He leaned against Ladon's soft chest, feeling his heart pounding, and then suddenly his arms were around him, lifting Mod up off the ground so their mouths could crash into one another.

Ladon was gentler and more restrained than Mod imagined, but they kissed with fervor, their tongues in sync. Enveloped in the arms of a strong man, Mod felt lighter than he ever had before, like he would float away if Ladon wasn't holding him here.

When they eventually parted, with Ladon setting Mod back on the ground, they were both breathless and wearing matching dazed smiles.

"We were meant to find each other, weren't we?" Mod realized.

Ladon nodded. "I think so, and I'm so glad we did."

"What do you suppose that means?" Mod asked. "Why would opposites of each other be fated to be together?"

"I don't know," Ladon admitted, and he cradled Mod's face tenderly in his large hand. "But like I said, we'll find out together."

CHAPTER ELEVEN

INVIDIA STOOD ON THE BANKS of the Certatio Lake with the sun setting behind him. It was unseasonably cold in the kingdom of Aemulatio, leaving much of the native wildlife in a prolonged hibernation, and it was oddly still and quiet.

Or at least it had been when Invidia had arrived at the shores of the lake with his pack of canu – the large demon dogs with leathery black skin and sharp fangs. Like him, the canu served Valefor, and while he'd been exiled, Invidia had made sure that he was left in possession of his Master's beasts.

That might have seemed solely due to his envious nature, but it was also pragmatic. None of his brethren seemed to care about Valefor's banishment, so if he was ever going to return to Cormundie, Invidia would have to be the one to help him.

And with all the others buddying up together (just because they didn't invite him to their little rendezvouses didn't mean he didn't hear about them) it was even more imperative that he had Valefor's authority behind him.

When his Master returned, he would become more powerful than ever before, and Invidia would be at his side, helping to craft the new covenant. He was determined to ensure that there would be no place for any of his other peccati or the disgusting virtus in the new world.

The canu had many wonderful abilities, but the one that came in the most handy was their tracking skills. Despite their canine appearance, their sense of smell was supernaturally intuitive. They could track *anything*, even something that seemed virtually odorless, like a golden dragon egg.

Apisius Valley was the very best place to find such an egg, but it was treacherous to get to because of the aggressive plants and insects.

That was yet another way that the Altered weather worked in Invidia's favor. Recent rainfalls had been unusually high in the valley, which had led to a few flash floods, and plants, animals, and dragon nests alike had all gotten swept away. Down to the lake.

The canu's sense of smell was so impressive that they could even track down a solitary dragon egg in the bottom of a lake.

They hadn't even been there that long when he heard one of the dogs let out a loud howl, alerting Invidia that they'd found what they'd been tracking.

The large beast lumbered up the shore, toward Invidia, and his wide muzzle hid the egg until he finally dropped it at Invidia's feet.

"Good boy," Invidia said as he picked up the egg. "I'll give you an extra goblin wing when we get home." As he grinned down at the glimmering shell, he changed his mind. "No, I'll give you a whole damned goblin."

Soon Invidia would put this in the hands of the obnoxious sorceress, and they would be one step closer to the sangcoranimilia and the return of their Master.

Cormundie

Desiderium

Bene

Otium

Volentia

Zelus

Auctoritas

Mitis

Insontia

Desperationis

Voracitas

Furorem

Sabrii

Aemulatio

Cupiditas

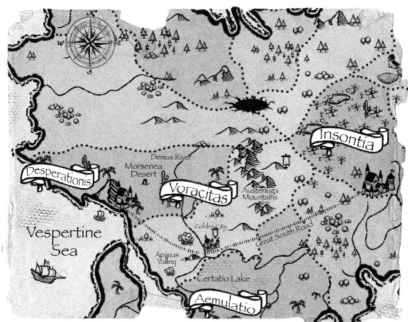

Desperationis

Insontia

Demius River

Morsenea Desert

Voracitas

Austeriuga Mountains

Vespertine Sea

Golden City

Great South Road

Apisius Valley

Certatio Lake

Aemulatio

Superbia

Seven Fallen Hearts

The saga continues in the next book. **Coming Soon**

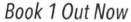

Book 1 Out Now

Book 2 Out Now

www.HockingBooks.com

ABOUT THE AUTHOR

AMANDA HOCKING is the author of over thirty-five novels, including the *New York Times* bestselling Trylle Saga and the indie bestseller My Blood Approves. Her love of pop culture and all things paranormal influence her writing. She spends her time in Minnesota, taking care of her menagerie of pets and working on her next book.

To learn more, please visit www.HockingBooks.com

Printed in Great Britain
by Amazon

45406174R00040